DEAR AUSTIN

Also by Elvira Woodruff:

Dear Levi: Letters from the Overland Trail

DEAR AUSTIN

LETTERS FROM THE UNDERGROUND RAILROAD

BY ELVIRA WOODRUFF

illustrated by Nancy Carpenter

SCHOLASTIC INC.

New York Toronto London Auckland Sydney
Mexico City New Delhi Hong Kong

ISBN 0-439-15814-1

Text copyright © 1998 by Elvira Woodruff. Illustrations copyright © 1998 by Nancy Carpenter. All rights reserved. Published by Scholastic Inc., 555 Broadway, New York, NY 10012, by arrangement with Alfred A. Knopf, Inc. SCHOLASTIC and associated logos are trademarks and/or registered trademarks of Scholastic Inc.

12 11 10 9 8 7 6 5 4 3   9/9 0 1 2 3 4/0

Printed in the U.S.A.   40

First Scholastic printing, November 1999

For Ann and Morry,
two of my nearest and dearest

with a nod to Jonathan Weiss and Joshua Sabatine,
two friends in the creek

Dear Austin,

Today seemed like Christmas on account of your letter arriving! Miss Amelia and I sat down together as she read it aloud. I especially liked the part about Reuben finding the rattlesnake in his boot and your sighting a grizzly bear. I closed my eyes when she read the part about your fishing on the lake. I could just picture the two of you netting the "biggest catch of your lives"! You sure were lucky to find Reuben on your way. Miss Amelia says he sounds like the kind of man a boy could learn a lot from. She hopes you learn some of his recipes. I told her you've got more on your mind than how to make an apple pie, what with a claim to settle and grizzly bears to look out for.

Sometimes I get so discouraged thinking about how the only way I ever get to see you is by closing my eyes. And I can't help wondering how different things would be if I had been able to come out to Oregon to join you like we planned. And to think that it's been two whole years since then! Why, I'll be eleven years old next month, near as old as you were when you left Pennsylvania with the wagon train. But you had better luck than me, Austin, and didn't come down with the consumption.

Miss Amelia still won't budge on the subject of me traveling now. She's always quoting old Doc Stanton, who says that consumption is nothing to fool with and that I should wait until next spring afore I tax my strength.

I keep telling Miss Amelia that I'm as strong as any boy I know and should be out with you and Reuben in Oregon on Pa's claim, but she shakes her head and her face gets all wrinkly with worry, and then she says what she always says:

"Levi Ives, are you trying to give a body heart palpitations? How would I stand it, sitting here in Pennsylvania worrying about you and your lungs and your daredevil ways out in that wilderness? When your ma died birthing you, I was at her side. And I promised her then that I'd look out for you. No, by goodness, you're going to stay right here with me until next spring, when your lungs are stronger, and maybe by then you'll have grown out of some of them wild ways."

I just roll my eyes when she carries on like that. I don't mind growing out of my britches or my shirt, but I don't intend on growing into some kind of sissy. Miss Amelia doesn't seem to understand that a boy's got to have some wildness in him if he's heading clear across the territories.

I think about all the walking you did with the wagon train, and I've decided to get my legs in shape for my turn. Yesterday I dared Willie Erlich and his cousins that Jupiter, Possum, and I could outrun them and Old Man Grissard's bull. So Jupiter and Possum are coming over and we're going to do some practice running out in the pasture afore we take on the bull Saturday morning.

Just how fast do you suppose a bull can run? I guess I'll find out soon enough. If he really gets going, we might light out of here and keep on running clear on out to Oregon! So if you see a cloud of dust, you'll know it's your brother and his two friends trying to steer clear of that old bull.

Of course, Miss Amelia don't know about the bull (I wouldn't want to get her heart all palpitated), so it's a secret run. Most everything Jupiter, Possum, and I do winds up secret, so we've started a club and we have a creed. It's a daredevil's creed, and I can't really say more than that on account of its being secret.

Thanks for sending that moon-faced button. Tell Reuben that Miss Amelia had to sew it onto a new coat for me, as I've outgrown my old one. But be sure to tell him that as big as I grow, I won't ever outgrow his button!

Your brother, Levi

P.S. You might remember how Possum is always catching frogs and toads down by his crick. Well, he has two new ones. One is a little toad he calls Hap, and the other is a big frog called Plug Ugly. Seems Possum's sister Maudee took one look at him and declared him to be "plug ugly," and the name just stuck. It's sort of like what happened to Possum. I finally learned how he got that nickname. When he was born, his older brother, Tom, said he looked like a little possum, and that's what everyone called him after that, excepting his ma, who insists on calling him Jonathan. Possum says that in the frog world "ugly" is beautiful and so Plug Ugly is real pleased with his new name.

Dear Austin,

I am happy to write that I have survived the attack of Old Man Grissard's bull! I didn't reckon on his temper turning so nasty all of a sudden (the bull, that is, not Old Man Grissard).

Austin, I got to admit I was afeared as the others were when I first laid eyes on that powerful beast! But as I am the leader of our club, I could not show it. The bull was standing in the pasture as calm as a turtle on a rock when Jupiter, Possum, and I sneaked up behind him.

"Be still, oh, mah heart!" Possum whispered as he stood gaping at the bull. This is Possum's favorite expression, ever since he heard it last year from a song-and-dance man who was traveling out West and had stopped in Sudbury to shoe his horse.

"Be still, oh, mah heart," Possum whispered again.

"You mean be still, oh, mah bull!" I said.

"He looks awfully big," Possum croaked. "I don't remember him looking so big or so mean."

"How can you tell he's mean," I whispered back, "when all's we can see is his rump?"

"It's a mean-looking rump, is how," Possum declared.

Jupiter nodded his head to agree. Jupiter never talks, you remember that, but Possum and I understand him just fine without words.

"I say we clear on out of here and forget the whole thing," Possum whispered, taking a step backward.

"And let Willie Erlich and his cousins think we're yeller on account of some old bull's rump scared us off?" I cried, grabbing him by the shirt sleeve.

"All right, all right." Possum sighed. "But couldn't we come back on Saturday when Willie and the others are here?"

I shook my head. "We know how fast Willie and his cousins can run, and we know we can beat 'em. But what we don't know is how fast *he* can run," I whispered, nodding toward the bull, whose rump hadn't budged since we first set eyes on it.

"Besides, it's all part of our training for the territories," I told them.

"They've got bulls out in the territories?" Possum whispered.

"Buffalo bulls," I reminded him. "All we've got to do today is get the bull to run and time him to see how fast he can go," I added, pulling a timepiece from my pocket. (I know it was wrong of me, Austin, but I had borrowed Miss Amelia's gold timepiece from her chest. You know the one—it used to be her pa's. I had every intention of returning it and only meant to borrow it to clock the bull.)

We decided that Possum and Jupiter would sneak around to the other side of the pasture and wave the piece of red cloth that I had also borrowed from Miss Amelia's chest.

"All you two have to do is wave the red flag," I explained. "And wait for the bull to start charging. Once he does, you hightail it back to the fence and climb over." Jupiter took the cloth that I had bunched up and tucked inside my shirt. As he opened it up, we all stared in astonishment.

Jupiter's eyes grew big and his mouth dropped open.

"Drawers!" Possum cried, as Jupiter held them up. "Ladies' drawers!"

I couldn't believe what I was seeing, for I had just grabbed this folded red material from Miss Amelia's trunk, thinking to use it as a flag. How was I to guess that Miss Amelia should have such things in her possession? And they were *red*, mind you!

Jupiter handed the dreaded object to Possum.

"I ain't waving no ladies' drawers," Possum declared, handing them back to me.

"All right," I said. "Forget the red flag. With your hair being so red, maybe that would be enough to attract him. All you have to do is make a ruckus in front of the bull to get his attention, and I'll wait here and keep the time."

They started for the other side of the pasture. Suddenly Possum turned and came running back, pulling something green out of his shirt.

"What's Plug Ugly doing here?" I groaned on seeing the frog in his hands.

"He hates for me to leave him behind," Possum admitted. "But he also hates when I run too fast. Gets him all shook up and ruins his digestion. Couldn't you hold him for me, Levi?"

I took Plug Ugly and dropped him into my shirt pocket.

I was waiting for the fellas to get to the other side of the pasture, and checking on the timepiece, when what does that durned frog do but jump out of my pocket! Not only that, but he jumps clear into the air and lands on the back of old Grissard's bull!

I don't think the bull felt Plug Ugly on him as much as he heard him. It was a real loud croak full of sass, as if to say he weren't afraid of nothing nor nobody. Now, that bull didn't take kindly to Plug Ugly's sassy croaks, I can tell you that. He spun around and began snorting some mean, angry bull snorts. Between all the snorting and croaking I was hoping that I could slip away unnoticed, but it was just my luck that that old bull caught sight of the red drawers in my hand! He figured it was me giving him all that sass and begging him to come at me!

"Hey, now, bull," I said, trying to calm him down. "It weren't me that was croaking..." But before I could explain, I got on one of those hiccupping jags that I always get when I'm real nervous. Anyway, the bull heard all that hiccupping, let out one more loud, angry snort, and began to charge!

I can't tell you how fast I was running, nor him neither, on account of I had dropped the timepiece by then. But I can tell you that I never moved faster! Luckily the bull was probably as old as Old Man Grissard himself and seemed to have trouble running, though what he lacked in speed he made up for in determination.

"Open the gate! Open the gate!" I yelled to Possum and Jupiter, who had come around to watch.

And to my great relief they did open the gate, but didn't have the sense to close it afore that bull came tearing through! He chased me all the way to the

Springers' orchard, where I was able to get a leg up an apple tree and climb to safety.

So as you may have guessed, I am at this writing in a heap of trouble, for that bull tore up the Springers' vegetable patch. It took Old Man Grissard and two other men most of the afternoon to rope the bull and direct him back to the pasture.

Jupiter, Possum, and I are to spend an entire day doing chores for Mrs. Springer to make up for her ruined beans. And next week we're to report to Old Man Grissard to muck out his stalls. Luckily Jupiter found Miss Amelia's timepiece, but it had a nasty dent in it from where the bull must have stepped on it.

I think Miss Amelia minded the "flag" more than the timepiece, for her cheeks were turning just as red as the drawers when I handed them back, and she looked as if she might be having those heart palpitations she's always going on about.

All this commotion landed me the punishment of Miss Amelia volunteering me to pluck chickens for the church picnic. She said all that plucking will give me time to "ruminate on changing my wild ways."

Old Man Grissard is so mad he's spitting nails, Mrs. Springer is still fuming over her bunch of beat-up beans, and Jupiter pulls a face every time he looks at me, on account of he's blaming me for all the chores we've got to do. Possum has gone into deep mourning over losing Plug Ugly, who we never did find.

I hope life is easier for you out in the territories. I suspect rattlesnakes and grizzly bears would prove relaxing after the troubles that I've braved right here in Sudbury!

Your brother, Levi

Dear Austin,

The big news in Sudbury is that Miller's store was broke into and robbed! The thieves took forty dollars from the safe, a box of hardtack, three hammers, a harness, and a case of Doctor Ditz's cough elixir, which also works for curing warts. Everyone in town is real jumpy, and we're all on the lookout for anyone with a strange look in his eye, a cough, or a wart. What I can't figure is how anyone could rob Miller's store without even touching the candy jars!

Last night I stunk so bad after mucking stalls all morning and plucking chickens for the church supper all afternoon, Miss Amelia wouldn't even let me into the kitchen to take my Friday-night bath. Jupiter was with me, on account of Fridays are his day to work for Miss Amelia. Do you remember his sister, Darcy? Well, she's two years younger and comes with him to do the churning and the wash for Widow Needly next door. You can always tell when Darcy is in the neighborhood because of her singing.

When she isn't singing, she's humming. Everyone calls her Darcy Nightingale on account of she sings like a nightingale, I guess.

Jupiter is eleven years old now and has a two-year-old hound dog by the name of Whistle. Even though Jupiter can't talk, he can whistle just fine, which is handy for calling his dog. Jupiter and Darcy work the rest of the week over at the Hepple farm. You may remember that their pa, Winston, is a farmhand there.

On Friday afternoon Miss Amelia sent Jupiter, Whistle, and me with the wagon to collect the chickens, and then we sat down and commenced plucking. I can't think of a chore I despise more than plucking chickens. Jupiter and I try to make a game out of it by racing each other to see who can pluck a bird the fastest. When we begin each race, Jupiter tucks a feather behind his ear. When I asked him why he did that, he pulled a rabbit's foot out of his pocket.

"Oh, for luck," I said. "Well, in that case, let's see if I get lucky enough to miss out on plucking for the next church supper." I stuck a handful of feathers behind both my ears, and Jupiter started to laugh. Jupe is the only person I know who can laugh without making a sound. I wish I had that talent, especially in church, where laughing is almost a sin.

By the time we were through we had plucked twenty birds, leaving us with a mess of feathers in our laps and the stink of dead chickens all over us. Jupiter helped me drag the tin tub out to the back porch, where we filled it from the well. After such a hot and sweaty job, the cool water felt so refreshing that we both jumped in, Jupe at one end and me at the other. Whistle took a good long drink from the tub afore lying down beside it.

The crickets had begun to chirp in the grass, an owl hooted from the willow tree, and the bullfrogs were having a croaking contest down by the pond. We had all the entertainment a body could want. It was a good night for stargazing, and Jupiter and I took turns pointing out our favorite stars.

Jupiter's quiet is full of meaning, once you understand him. His eyes tell me more than most folks can with words. I know all of his expressions, and it's as if I can hear what he's saying in his silence.

Miss Amelia said that Jupiter saw some terrible things happen to his mama in the slave quarters down in Maryland, afore he could learn to talk, and it frightened the words right out of him. Darcy must have missed seeing those things, for she talks more than anybody I know. And when she isn't talking, she's singing.

But Jupiter and I don't need talking or singing to have a good time. I would have been content to sit there soaking and stargazing for an hour or more, but I suddenly spotted a suspicious light behind Preacher Tully's smokehouse—not starlight but lantern light.

"Hey, Jupe," I whispered. "Do you see that light back of Tully's smokehouse?"

But Jupiter just shrugged as if it weren't nothing to bother about. I wasn't so sure.

So of course after my bath, my prayers, and my promises to Miss Amelia to "curb my wild ways and try to act more responsible," I tied a rope to my bedpost and dropped it out my window.

That's all I have time to write you now, on account of my time is taken up with a new punishment Miss Amelia dreamed up after she learned I had slipped out of the house last night. For now I will just say that I have been given the most torturous punishment a boy could imagine, and if I live through it I will write you further about the night which cost me so dearly.

Your about-to-be-tortured brother, Levi

Dear Austin,

I have survived my latest punishment, but only bare-ly. I'll relate the grim details for you, but first let me explain how it all came about.

It began with my spying that light back of Preacher Tully's smokehouse on Friday night and deciding to lower myself out my bedroom window.

Now, I know what you might be thinking, Austin, but I can honestly say that my sneaking out of the house had nothing to do with wildness and every-thing to do with responsibility. For it's part of our club's creed that if something suspicious is going on, it's up to the club to investigate it. What with the rob-bery at Miller's store and a thief full of warts on the loose, I just had to do the responsible thing and lead the investigation.

I headed as fast as I could for Possum's house. (Jupiter's pa had come for him in the wagon to take him home.) Luckily there is a big oak tree standing under Possum's bedroom window. I tossed up a pebble to wake him, and he was quick to climb down the tree to join me.

We headed for the woods that would take us to Tully's smokehouse. The moon was big and bright enough to light our way, and the pine needles on the ground felt soft as a carpet under our bare feet. There's something special about walking through the woods when it's all shadows and moonlight.

We stopped by the crick to check Possum's frog houses. He's made them all along the bank. They're holes he's dug into the mud and covered with twigs and leaves. We were hoping that Plug Ugly might find his way back to his house, which was the biggest, but there was no sign of him.

Then we hung around the crick making leaf boats and having races. The moonlight was so bright we could see clear downstream to the bridge. When we smelled a skunk, we decided to get out of there fast and headed home.

We were having such a fine time that we never did see to the light behind Tully's smokehouse. But I intend to get to the bottom of this before the summer is over. All in all it was a good night, until I climbed back up to my room to find Miss Amelia there waiting for me! It was just my luck that she had woken up in the middle of the night with a misery in her neck and noticed that I wasn't in my bed. For this small offense, Miss Amelia has burdened me with a punishment so cruel and horrible, I wonder if I shall live through it.

I am to take dancing lessons!

Austin, I fear Miss Amelia is developing a real cruel streak in her, and with you gone, I am left to suffer alone under it! Dancing lessons at prissy Mrs. Simpson's! Why, going up against Old Man Grissard's bull was a piece of cake by comparison.

Your aggrieved brother, Levi

Dear Austin,

Today started off bad, took a turn for the worse, and ended up pretty near perfect. I woke up to find Essie in a bad mood. You know our Essie is the best-natured cow there ever was, but I could tell right away that something was wrong this morning, for when I put my bucket down beside her, she kicked it hard. I shouldn't have ignored that kick, but I did, and when I went to pull on her teat to let down her milk, she near kicked the bucket across the barn!

Miss Amelia said Essie most likely was suffering one of her spells, and I had to pick her some comfrey leaves to make up a poultice. As the day wore on, I was wishing that Essie's kick had knocked me instead of the bucket across the barn, so's I wouldn't have to go to the dreaded dancing lessons that afternoon. The whole rest of the morning was ruined, on account of I was counting the hours and minutes until Miss Amelia called me to come and "wash."

That was the first torture. She scrubbed my fingernails with pine-tar soap and dug out the dirt with a nasty little pick for what seemed like hours. When I complained that they didn't even look like my fingers anymore, Miss Amelia just smiled and kept on scrubbing. Next I had to get into a collared shirt that had been starched so stiff you could have sailed me down the crick on it.

Of course I had to put on my Sunday shoes, and Miss Amelia showed no sympathy for my squashed toes. As if this weren't enough for a boy to suffer through, my head was attacked next.

Miss Amelia moaned how she forgot to buy the hair pomade down at Miller's store, but she supposed a little lard would do. Finally she stood me in front of her looking glass and smiled with satisfaction.

"There now." She sighed. "How do you feel?"

I stood there staring into the glass, all scrubbed, picked over, collared, squashed, and slicked down with lard.

"Miserable," I muttered through clenched teeth. "Jest plain miserable."

But that didn't waver Miss Amelia from her mission. She told me how she hoped that I would be a big success at Mrs. Simpson's. And looking at me now, she didn't see any reason why I shouldn't be. "This will be your moment," she declared. "Your moment to shine."

"If I have to go through all this pain to have one shining moment," I told her, "I'd as soon keep my moments on the dull side."

"Promise me," she insisted. "Promise me you'll act like a gentleman." So of course I had to promise, 'cause even though Miss Amelia ain't really our ma, she fusses over me the same as any ma would. And I guess I can't complain. It's not every person who'll take in a boy with wild ways.

When we finally did arrive at Mrs. Simpson's, we found five girls and only three boys in the dancing group. There were the three sorry-looking Podorsky sisters, all sour-faced and pouty, little Addie Rudder, who's only seven years old, and Tessa Buckman, who is probably the most beautiful girl in all of Sudbury, maybe in all of Pennsylvania! I felt a powerful round of hiccups coming on just looking at her.

Lester Minter, Henry Fenton, and I made up the boys. Henry had been clever enough to take music lessons, which got him out of dancing, as he was needed to play the fiddle. That left Lester and me to be tortured. Lester, being the kind of boy who was brought up on prunes and proverbs, is known for two specialties. His spelling ability (he wins every spelling bee) and his scab picking. Lester is never without a scab he can pick. In the summer he's got them mostly on his knees, but when cool weather comes and his legs are covered, he starts in on his arms. He takes his time and goes at it real slow. But he wasn't picking any scabs on his legs today, for his ma was bragging to Miss Amelia and Mrs. Simpson how she had gotten Lester a pair of fancy store-bought britches "special for the occasion."

"Why, he's turned out like a perfect little gentleman," Mrs. Simpson cooed. All the girls were giggling and smiling (even Tessa Buckman) as if Lester the Scab Picker had somehow been turned into Lester the Prince! Lester was swelling like a bullfrog, and his mother was beside herself with pride.

I felt bad for Miss Amelia, who kept shooting me withering looks as she sat waiting for my shining moment to happen. I wouldn't want anything like fancy store-bought britches for myself, of course, but for Miss Amelia's sake, and maybe even Tessa Buckman's, I almost wished I had me a pair!

Later Mrs. Simpson was pairing us up, and didn't she pick the most beautiful girl in the room for the bullfrog's partner. You should have seen Lester gloat as he took Tessa Buckman's hand.

Naturally, as things were going from bad to worse, I was paired with Margaret Podorsky. Skinny old Margaret Podorsky never smiles and is in the habit of chewing on the ends of her braids, leaving her hair ribbons all slimy with spit. If that ain't attractive enough, she's got the stink of camphor on her, as her ma still rubs her thumbs with some evil-smelling concoction so she won't suck them, even though she's nearly ten years old.

I gritted my teeth, hiccupped, and took Margaret's stinky hand. While Mrs. Simpson was explaining about "twirling your partners," a big bottle fly flew in from the window and buzzed our heads. My hair was so thick with lard, didn't that fly dive down and land right on the top of my head! To make things worse, it got stuck in the lard and couldn't take off.

Of course Lester, being the "perfect little gentleman," couldn't let this go unnoticed and called to Tessa Buckman to "take a look at Levi the Fly Catcher." Even Henry was giggling as he played.

I shot Lester a dirty look, and as I twirled Margaret in a turnabout, I reached with my free hand and grabbed for the fly, pulling it off my head. Of course I knew better than to wipe it and the glob of lard from my fingers on my clean britches, so I reached over and used the back of Margaret's dress as she spun around. This caused a loud shriek from Mrs. Simpson. How'd I know that she'd be looking just then? Somehow I don't think this was the shining moment that Miss Amelia was dreaming about.

The rest of the lesson was just plain tiresome, what with all the bowing and the two steps forward and two steps back.

That night, Possum came to sleep over, and guess who came with him? Plug Ugly! Didn't he find his way back to his frog house by the crick!

I perked up considerable on hearing this news and seeing Plug Ugly's ugly face. Possum has a good little cage made of twigs for him. We three slept out in the hayloft. We stayed up late looking at the stars and talking about frogs and flies and Plug Ugly's bumpy back. (He's got more bumps on it than any frog Possum's ever caught.)

We talked a lot about our club and how we had to work harder at being alert, on account of it could be downright dangerous if we weren't. I wish you were here and could be in our club, Austin, 'cause you know all about being a real daredevil. If you were here, I don't think there would be anybody who'd object to making you president of the club, what with all the danger you faced on the wagon train. But with you so far off, I guess I'll have to keep the job. Possum says that I make a pretty good president, 'cepting for my hiccups. It was such a good night, I almost forgot about my punishing day.

I was trying to recall what kind of punishments you had when you lived at home, Austin, and try as I might, I couldn't remember any. I don't know how you managed to ward them off so well. I seem to have a natural talent for attracting them. I suppose it has something to do with my being so responsible.

I know you are busy working the claim, but if you find the time, I'd sure like to hear from you. There may be an entire country separating us, Austin, but I know I can always tell my troubles to you. And sometimes that makes you seem mighty close.

Your brother, Levi

Dear Austin,

Possum, Jupiter, and I have had our first swim over at the swimming hole. The water was cold at first, but we warmed up, jumping off the rope swing. Harley Rush showed up and began to climb the hillside to Widow's Rock. You know how high that is, Austin. Only the best divers dare to go off it. When Harley got to the top, he called down to us, daring us to dive. We didn't pay him any mind until we heard a familiar bark and looked up to see Whistle coming round behind him! Whistle must have followed Harley up the trail while we were in the water.

Harley's bigger and stronger than the three of us put together. He's also got a real mean streak in him, and when he caught sight of Whistle, he pulled a piece of beef jerky from his pocket and held it out for him. Jupiter, Possum, and I were all whistling for Whistle to come down. But that hound loves two things in this world: Jupiter and beef jerky. And as good as Jupiter must smell to him, I guess beef jerky just smells better.

When he put his nose in Harley's hand, Harley wrapped his arms around him and laughed.

"Looks like this dog is the only one brave enough to take my dare and dive off Widow's Rock," he yelled down to us.

"Leave him be, Harley," I shouted back up.

"I'll leave him be if one of you comes on up and takes his place. But if you don't dive, the dog does," he threatened, holding Whistle out over the water. None of us doubted he'd do it.

I started to swim for the bank, but Jupiter grabbed on to my arm and pulled me back. His jaw was clenched shut and his eyes were stony with determination. I knew he'd made up his mind to go. Possum and I watched as he climbed out of the water, got into his britches, and made his way up the trail to Widow's Rock. When he got to the top, he stopped.

I held my breath, wondering what he'd do next, on account of I know that Jupiter is scared to death of high places. When he sits in the hayloft, he never goes near the window or climbs up to the rafters the way Possum and I sometimes do.

Jupiter lifted his arms over his head. Everyone grew silent as he closed his eyes. We waited. And waited, and waited some more.

"If you ain't going to do it, move over and let your dog here have a go at it," Harley finally declared. "I ain't waiting all day."

Jupiter took a step forward, and afore I knew it he had jumped! He shot down like a bullet to the bottom, and was pretty shook up when he surfaced, but Possum and I got ahold of him and helped him to the bank. We told him it was the bravest thing we ever saw anybody do!

Whistle had come back down the trail after Harley let him go, and he was licking Jupiter's face, thanking him, I suppose, for being brave enough to jump off of Widow's Rock.

Walking through the woods on our way home, we came upon some good lengths of hickory that somebody had cut and left. So we grabbed some rods and decided to make walking sticks out of them when we got home.

The next day when Jupiter's pa, Winston, was

driving to the feed mill, he stopped his wagon by the woodshed to talk to Jupiter and me. Winston is a broad-shouldered man—do you remember?—with a row of pink stripes running down the side of his dark-skinned face. Jupiter's face is blacker than his father's but free of stripes, and Winston says that he intends to see that it stays that way.

Folks tell how Winston got those scars afore he got his freedom, when he was a slave. I like Jupiter's pa, 'cause he always smiles when he sees us and asks, "How you menfolk doing today?"

When he asked us this afternoon, I told him how we wanted to do some whittling, as we had some hickory cut.

"A good whittler needs two things," Winston said, taking a length of hickory from my hand. "First, you needs patience, 'cause you can't hurry de wood. And second, you needs what dey call a 'whittler's eye.'"

Jupiter and I looked at each other and squinted our eyes. "Like this?" I asked.

Winston laughed and shook his head. Winston laughs real easy, especially when he's around menfolk like Jupiter and me. "Unless you have a notion to lose a few fingers, I think it best if you keeps your eyes open," he said. "With a whittler's eye, a body can see clear through de wood to de thing it is he wants to whittle. Once you can see that," he said, "all you have to do is shave off de extra wood around it."

Jupiter and I got out our knives and stared hard at the hickory rods we had chosen. I am making a walking stick for Reuben, since you said he likes to wander through the woods picking berries and leaves for his concoctions. I will bring it with me on the wagon train next spring. I wanted to fashion the head of a pirate for the handle. But so far it looks more like a turnip with a nose!

Jupiter's stick is coming out much better than mine. He is making a smaller walking stick for his sister, Darcy. He's decided that the top of the stick should be shaped like a bird, a nightingale. I wish you could see the two little wings he's carved. They look so light and feathery that you'd expect them to start flapping!

I wonder what Darcy will say when she sees her

stick. I guess she'll probably start to sing! I don't imagine Reuben will sing when he sees old turnip head, but I hope he likes his stick enough to make use of it.

Your brother, Levi

Dear Austin,

I am still being tortured with dancing lessons, but I've been bearing up as best I can. The only good part is when I get Tessa Buckman as my partner. Yesterday I had no flies on my head and only stepped on her feet twice, so I think I made a fair impression.

This is a short letter, as I have been helping Possum and his pa bring in their hay, and I am mighty tuckered out at the end of the day. We're not big enough yet for pitching, so Possum and I have been raking. Today Possum's pa showed us how to use the big bullrakes. It was tricky at first, but we finally got the hang of it and raked right alongside Nat, the hired man. Nat's all right, 'cepting he ate some beans that were talking behind his back and we had to keep our distance!

We've been holding our club meetings up in Possum's barn. Since we've decided to make you an honorary member, Austin, I guess it's all right for me to tell you what we're planning. First off, we're going to hunt down the thieves that got away from Miller's store. Next we're going to find out about the mysterious light at Preacher Tully's place. And last we're going to find a remedy to stop hiccups. Possum and Jupiter don't mind my affliction so much, but if we decide to take in new members, well, I just figure it would look more dignified if our president could face danger without hiccupping.

So I'm needing your help, Austin, not with tracking down the thieves or uncovering the mystery of the light. Those will be easy tasks. But curing my hiccups—now, that's another matter altogether. It's akin to trying to put socks on a rooster. I just don't know if it can be done. Miss Amelia says that I'll outgrow the habit, but I was hoping you'd have some suggestions until I do.

Last night I had a bad nightmare. I dreamed that I found the thieves. But I was hiccupping so much that they just laughed and picked me up and carried me to Widow's Rock and threw me off. Do you ever have nightmares, Austin? Do you think I can outgrow them, too?

Your brother, Levi

Dear Austin,

It was good to get your letter. Thank Reuben for the hiccup cure. Jupiter and I spent all afternoon picking elderberries and pine needles for the tea. I drank five cups and didn't hiccup once (of course, I wasn't nervous about anything at the time, so I guess I'll just have to wait till I am and see what happens). Miss Amelia wanted me to write and ask if Reuben has a favorite pie recipe he would be willing to share. The pie social is coming up, and Miss Amelia is determined to win first place this year. She says that your Reuben is "a gem," on account of he knows all about making good pies and curing the hiccups.

Today as Possum and I were weeding the garden, we heard Darcy singing as usual out back in Widow Needly's summer kitchen. But what wasn't usual was the song she was singing. "Add two cups flour, half a cup lard, half a cup cornmeal…" It was the flapjack recipe from the widow's recipe book! Darcy, who's never been to a proper school, was reading! Miss

Amelia says that down in Maryland where Jupiter and Darcy were born, it is against the law to teach a slave to read or write. Our state of Pennsylvania is free, but the trouble is there are no schools for coloreds close by.

Later when Nelly Hepple came over with the wool she had spun for Miss Amelia, she stopped in the yard to talk to Possum and me. I asked Nelly if she knew about Darcy's reading. She said that Darcy had been pleading to learn to read, so Nelly's older sister Hannah had been teaching her, using the family Bible. Nelly said that once Darcy got the hang of reading, she didn't want to stop.

I can't think why Darcy should not be allowed to learn to read and why she's got to plead to do it. There's plenty in my class who would plead *not* to do their schoolwork. I don't know how there can be a law that keeps folks from learning. I wonder at the men who thought up such a law and why they were so determined to keep a young girl from reading the Bible—just because of the color of her skin. It makes no sense, Austin.

I never heard anybody make a song out of a recipe for flapjacks, and when Darcy started to sing it again, Nelly had to use her handkerchief to wipe her eyes, on account of Darcy had made "two cups flour and half a cup lard" into the sweetest, saddest song you ever heard.

Sometimes I can't help thinking about Darcy and Jupiter and how different their lives are from mine, all because of what they look like. I think about the nightmares I've been having, almost every night, and wonder what kind of nightmares Jupe must have.

Your brother, Levi

P.S. Miss Amelia wrote down her recipe for teacup pudding, and so I am including it. She says to tell Reuben that if he soaks the raisins in brandy, they will plump up nice.

Dear Austin,

Today Possum and I were over at Miller's store waiting for Miss Amelia to do her shopping. The usual bunch of old men were sitting out on the porch talking, chewing, spitting, and puffing on their pipes. When Possum and I sat down on the porch steps to eat our rock candy, we heard Old Man Potts going on about the new coach due in from Richmond.

"They say it makes twelve miles an hour!" he claimed.

"Are you sure you're not confusing it with an iron horse?" Mr. Tanner asked.

"I'm not talking about the railroad, Jeb. I'm talking about a regular coach with four horses. Living, breathing horses."

"Not living for long, traveling at twelve miles an hour!" Mr. Tanner snorted. "What's everybody in such a durned hurry for, anyway? They're liable to addle their brains moving at those speeds."

"Expecting *that* one ought to quicken his step,"

Old Man Potts said with a nod toward the street. I looked up to see Winston loading a wagon in front of the feed mill.

"Why is that?" Mr. Tanner asked.

"Word is that a couple of slave catchers are due in on this coach," Old Man Potts said. "And you know how they hate to return empty-handed."

"But he's not a slave," I spoke up. "Winston is a free man. He has it in writing."

Old Man Potts looked over at me and shook his head. "I don't expect those slave catchers will be much interested in writing, son. My guess is they're interested in one thing and that's color. They're looking for black hides."

I have to tell you, Austin, I felt my rock candy stick in my throat on hearing those last words of his.

"You can't blame the plantation owners," someone else was saying. "What with so many slaves running off, why, it's liable to ruin them."

"I still contend it's a sinful business." Mr. Farber sighed.

"You're right on half a count," Old Man Potts

said, spitting a wad of juice from his mouth. "It is *business*. Those cotton men are only protecting their investments. And with that Fugitive Slave Law passed in '50, why, they've got every legal right to take back what belongs to them by law."

"They may have the law on their side," Mr. Farber said, "but the law hasn't stopped the Underground Railroad. And once a slave gets a ticket north on that train, there's no stopping him."

Miss Amelia called from inside the store just then for Possum and me to fetch her baskets. All the way home Possum and I kept our eyes on the ground, wondering about this Underground Railroad. Possum even tried putting his ear to the dirt, hoping to hear the iron horse's engine, but he couldn't hear anything excepting dirt, which as you know is pretty quiet.

I am worried about those slave catchers and wonder why they are looking for slaves above ground and not below. I suspect they are looking for some kind of secret door that leads to the Underground Railroad. I hope they leave Jupiter's pa alone.

Tomorrow Jupiter and I are going to make up another batch of Reuben's hiccup remedy tea. Possum found an old whiskey flask in his grandpa's attic. We're going to fill it with the tea, and that way I can keep it on me for emergencies. Best be getting to bed, as my lamp is low on oil.

Your brother, Levi

Dear Austin,

I have some news about the Underground Railroad. I found out at dinner that it is not underground at all! And not even a railroad! When I asked Miss Amelia about it, she seemed real surprised. I told her what I had heard at Miller's store and she said that there were no tracks underground and no train! She said that there were just people helping people to freedom. The Underground Railroad is a secret network of folks who use their houses to hide slaves who are running north out of slavery.

When I told her what Old Man Potts had said about the law being on the side of the slave catchers, Miss Amelia frowned. "Sometimes," she said, "a body has to follow the laws of their heart. If in your heart you know a law to be bad and to cause suffering, then you must follow the course of good, even if it goes against the law of the land. That is what the men and women who are working to free the slaves are doing."

"Women?" I asked, for I was surprised that there would be any women working on this railroad.

Miss Amelia went on to tell me about a brave "conductor," a slave named Harriet Tubman. She said this woman was so brave that people call her Moses, like from the Bible. She has a price on her head for taking slaves out of slavery down south and bringing them up north on the Underground Railroad.

When I asked Miss Amelia how it was she knew so much about this Underground Railroad, she said we had talked enough and the ash bucket needed emptying. That's what she always says when she wants to change the subject. I can't tell you how many times I've had to empty that ash bucket when it weren't nearly full!

Later that evening, Possum, Jupiter, and I were sitting up in the hayloft working on our whittling. Darcy Nightingale started to climb the ladder to fetch Jupiter to walk her home. It was a close call, for she almost caught sight of the stick Jupiter is making for her. If it weren't for Possum throwing a horse blanket over Jupiter's lap, Darcy would have seen it for sure.

"Ain't no girls allowed up here," I told her. She huffed and puffed and said she wouldn't bother us. And afore I knew it, she had set herself down in the straw beside the loft window and was humming a tune as she swung her legs over the window ledge.

Jupiter was helping me with old turnip head. We were trying to get his features to look less vegetable and more human, but we weren't having much success. Darcy started asking all kinds of questions, talking and singing and jabbering away. I finally had to tell her to "hush up." Just as she did, we heard the barn owl hoot up in the rafters, and as we all turned to look we saw it swoop down into the barn and snatch up a mouse that was running out of Essie's stall. The mouse was wiggling and struggling to free itself, but it was no match for the death grip of that owl.

Darcy covered her face with her hands and didn't make a peep after that. She's got a big mouth for a little girl, but I suppose her heart's just as big, especially when it comes to tiny critters.

I'm sitting at the kitchen table as I write this. And the room is full of our favorite smell. Do you remember what that was? Warm cherry pie! There are four pies cooling in the pie safe. Miss Amelia has taken to baking for Preacher Tully and his old father, who lives with him. Seems she can't bake them just one pie but insists on two and sometimes three! Possum says that maybe Miss Amelia is sweet on the preacher. Either that or she's trying to bake herself into heaven!

I wish you were here, Austin, so we could finish off one of these pies together the way we used to. Guess I'll just have to work on one alone! I hope Reuben is baking something special for you right now.

Your about-to-be-grinning brother, Levi

Dear Austin,

The only news I have to tell you is that there's been another robbery in Sudbury! Charlie's blacksmith shed was broken into and some of his best irons were stolen. Charlie's daughter Anna saw the thieves from her bedroom window and woke up the rest of the house. By the time Charlie got to the shed, the thieves had gone. Anna did get a look at them, but she couldn't make out their faces, it being so dark. What she could see, though, was that there were two of them, one tall and the other short.

Jupiter, Possum, and I have been working on our whittling up in the hayloft. Ever since she saw the barn owl kill that mouse, Darcy hasn't bothered us. She's so afraid of the owl that she won't even step into the barn. When she comes for Jupiter, she stands outside and calls up to him. If we see that she's getting braver and coming closer, we just start hooting and she runs away!

I was telling Jupiter and Possum what I had found out about the Underground Railroad, and Jupiter's eyes got mighty big. I asked him if he knew any more about it, but he just shrugged as if he didn't. Possum had other things on his mind—namely, worms. When Possum gets on a new subject, he'll go on about it for days.

The subject of worms is what he's been stuck on all week. He said he'd been studying them, and he figures that they're smarter than dogs. I said they weren't. And I went on to say that it would take a mighty dumb person to consider a worm smart.

Jupiter grinned and pointed to Possum. He was only fooling, but Possum didn't take it that way. He said that neither of us had "the brains God gave a squirrel" and marched off home.

Possum's got a short fuse, and when he's proved wrong, it's like to blow. I expect he'll get over it in a few days' time.

Everybody is jumpier than ever on account of the robbery, and I now sleep with my slingshot under my pillow. I wish the thieves would come around our place and I had a shot at them.

Your brother, Levi

Dear Austin,

Something bad happened yesterday, and it was all my fault. I keep thinking, If only I could take it back. Have you ever felt this way, Austin?

Sometimes I wish that you weren't clear across the country but rather home with me here in Sudbury. Because sometimes I come upon things that I just can't figure out on my own.

Jupiter, Possum, and I were out in front of the house having a critters contest. There was frog jumping, turtle crawling, and worm slinking. We had lined all the critters up and were running races. Most of the contestants were performing admirably, 'cepting the worms. They kept curling up and didn't seem especially interested in the notion of speed. Anyway, we were watching the worms and waiting for them to straighten out and move when Darcy Nightingale came over from Widow Needly's place to fetch some molasses. She went into the house and came out to wait while Miss Amelia poured the molasses into a jar.

Darcy was humming as usual, but she looked different somehow, and when I mentioned this she began to grin.

"Is it her dress, Jupe?" I asked. "Is she wearing a new dress?"

Jupiter shook his head.

"Seems like I was born in this old blue linsey-woolsey," Darcy said. "Miss Pearly complains every time she's got to let it down or out."

I stared hard at her, and she started to giggle.

"It's mah new hair ribbons," she answered proudly, bringing her hand to her head. That's when I noticed the yellow material tied in little bows all over her head.

"Miss Pearly made herself some new curtains yesterday, and she said I could have de scraps that were too small to go in her quilting basket," explained Darcy.

"Be still, oh, mah heart!" Possum teased.

But Darcy didn't pay him any mind. She was beaming with pride when Miss Amelia came out with the molasses and told her how becoming she looked in yellow.

"It's mah favorite color," Darcy admitted, "same as buttercups. I fixed myself up special on account of I'm going to pay a visit to mah friend Neddy, who's feeling poorly with de whooping cough." She leaned over to show us the little bunch of buttercups she had pinned to the frayed collar of her worn blue dress.

Jupiter, Possum, and I just shrugged, not being too impressed with buttercups. Miss Amelia smiled and went back into the house. Darcy stood talking about buttercups and telling us how she was going to pick a bunch for Neddy.

"Why is it that people always bring flowers when a body takes sick?" Possum asked as he nudged one of the worms with his finger.

"Or when a body dies," I said, looking over at Jupiter, who was lying on his back playing dead.

"'Cause buttercups always cheer a body up," Darcy replied, giving her brother a poke.

"Not a dead body," I told her.

"I'd think a licorice stick could cheer up a live body more than some old buttercups," Possum said.

Darcy frowned. "I reckon Neddy would be

pleased to git a stick of licorice, but I don't have de penny to buy it with."

"Maybe you could give her something else," I said.

Darcy twisted her torn ribbons as she tried to think.

Jupiter sat up and put his fingers over Darcy's throat. It's what he does when he wants to hear a song.

"Jupiter's right," I said. "Why don't you sing Neddy one of your songs?"

"But she's heard all I know," Darcy moaned.

I supposed she was right. Hearing an old song wouldn't be as special as hearing one brand new. We all hung around the porch pondering the situation, when suddenly I had an idea. "Why don't you come on over to Mrs. Simpson's this afternoon around three o'clock? Henry Fenton plays all kinds of tunes on his fiddle for our dancing lessons. All you have to do is sit outside Mrs. Simpson's window and listen. You could make up your own words and even put Neddy in the song if you like."

We all agreed that this was a good idea, and

Darcy thanked me and said she would be by. So that afternoon, while Margaret Podorsky and I were waltzing beside Mrs. Simpson's window, I heard a familiar voice singing outside.

Mrs. Simpson heard it too, and she stuck her head out the window to find Darcy Nightingale and her friend Etta May singing along with the music, making up the words as they went.

"Be off with you now! Scat!" Mrs. Simpson snapped as she slammed the window shut. You would have thought she was shooing away a couple of cats. Darcy and Etta May took off running, but later on when Henry was playing the last reel, I spied a headful of yellow ribbons back under the other window that was still open.

Mrs. Simpson didn't slam the window shut this time but rather went tearing for the door instead. I tried to warn Darcy, but it was too late, for Mrs. Simpson had gotten ahold of her arm. Etta May was lucky enough to get away and took off running down the street. Henry stopped playing, and we all stood frozen at the open window, watching.

"This is a respectable house," Mrs. Simpson fumed as she shook Darcy's arm.

"I didn't mean no harm," Darcy tried to explain.

"The harm is that you are here at all," Mrs. Simpson told her. "Why, I can't have a pack of pickaninnies hanging around, or proper folks wouldn't let their children come for lessons. So don't let me find you under my windows again. You keep yourself and your kind away from decent folks, or you'll find yourself singing in a cotton field under the shadow of a cat-o'-nine-tails, where you belong..."

Mrs. Simpson went on railing, but I couldn't hear any more of the hateful words she was spitting out. All I could hear was the pounding of my heart as I watched the tears well up in Darcy's eyes. She took notice of me then and dropped her head. The sight of those little yellow ribbons bobbing up and down as she stood trembling afore us filled me with shame.

I felt my throat tightening as I watched Mrs. Simpson roughly let go of her arm. Darcy turned and began to run, but she wasn't looking where she was going and she tripped in a rut in the street.

When muddy water from the rut splashed up on her dress, Lester Minter began to snicker. I grabbed him by the shirt and he began to holler. That's when Mrs. Simpson came in and pulled us apart.

After hearing Mrs. Simpson's account of my "attack on Lester," Miss Amelia's face grew red with embarrassment. I supposed I was in for another round of punishments, but when I explained things to Miss Amelia later at home, she had no words of rebuke for me at all. Instead she seemed real sad, but as sad as Miss Amelia's eyes became, they weren't nothing compared with the misery in Darcy Nightingale's look. You should have seen those eyes, Austin, and those little yellow buttercups on her collar all splattered with mud. I wonder if she can ever forgive me...

Your brother, Levi

Dear Austin,

Things are real quiet here, and there's not much to write you. We had a club meeting yesterday and decided to do some investigating. We went over to Charlie the blacksmith's place to see if we could find any clues to the robbery. Jupiter found an old horseshoe behind the shed, and Possum found a patch of poison ivy just beyond that. He walked smack into it afore he realized what it was. Do you remember how Possum puffs all up whenever he gets into poison? Well, he was so sure he was going to puff up again that we had to call off the investigation.

The three of us went back to our hayloft to wait for it to happen. We sat around for a good half hour just waiting and watching for Possum's puffin' to commence. But except for a little itching he looked the same, and we decided to take up our whittling while we waited. Jupiter's stick is almost finished. There is no singing to be heard coming from Widow Needly's summer kitchen, and it don't seem natural.

I couldn't stop thinking about Darcy, and so as we sat there whittling, I told Jupiter how I felt like what had happened to Darcy was all my fault and I hoped she would forgive me. He didn't look me in the eye but instead just kept working on his stick.

Miss Amelia says that there are all kinds of people in the world and that Mrs. Simpson is of the ignorant variety. Miss Amelia says that ignorance breeds hate, and hate can cause a lot of suffering. She has decided that it would be best not to be around such hateful ignorance, so I am not to return to my dancing lessons! Any other time I would be dancing for joy at this news, but somehow I can't even seem to smile, not with it being so quiet around here.

Your brother, Levi

Dear Austin,

Today was the strangest day, though it started out normal enough. Possum and I went over to the barn raising at the Fenton farm. I took along my flask of hiccup remedy just in case. You know it's a four-mile walk to the Fentons', and the road sure is hot and dusty this time of year. But lots of folks were there with picnic baskets full of good food. Mr. Sipes made some tasty root beer, and a good taffy pull was going on.

Angus Ripley and his cousin Ellis found some fair-size tobacco butts over by where the men were unloading timber, and they stowed them in their pockets. On our way home we stopped off at the swimming hole before the bend in the river and met Angus and some of the others there.

They were smoking the butts, and little Georgie Nestor was gagging and turning green, and they had to dump him in the water to get him to stop.

We met Possum's sister Maudee back on the

road. She wanted to walk home with us but insisted on stopping every two feet on account of a splinter she had in her foot. We finally had to stop and get it out with the pin that was holding up Possum's britches. I had to hold up his britches while he dug out the splinter. Anyway, by the time we got to Mud Run Road it was almost dark. That's when things started turning strange, Austin.

We were walking as fast as we could when we saw a light coming from behind Preacher Tully's smokehouse. This was the second time I had seen that light, and it just didn't make sense to me. The ground is swampy back there, and the preacher is not a hunter. So whose light could it be? And what were they doing out there? Following the club creed, I knew I'd have to do the responsible thing once again and get to the bottom of things.

We decided to head over to the smokehouse through the woods, since it was on our way home anyway. The moon gave us plenty of light.

All of a sudden Maudee, who was behind us, let out a scream that pretty near scared us out of our skins!

Possum and I both turned around to see a big old copperhead stretching out from behind a gooseberry bush. He was fixing his sights on Maudee's foot!

What happened next was so surprising it still seems like some kind of dream, for what should come flying out of the bushes but a hatchet, which took that snake's head clear off!

"What you all doing out here in dese parts so late?" a deep voice rose out of the bushes. A fit of hiccups had come on me afore I could answer. As I was reaching for the flask in my back pocket, I was relieved to see that it was only Winston and Jupiter stepping out afore us. I took a swig of tea and smiled, but they didn't smile back.

"We were just cutting through the woods on our way home," I said, suddenly noticing the rifle in Winston's hands.

"Well, that's one dangerous thing to be doing after dark," Winston snapped. "A body could get hisself shot."

"Shot?" Maudee shuddered beside me.

"Surely so," Winston replied. "Men be out hunting possum this time of night. Not no time for chilrens to be walking about."

I felt a shiver run through me. I had never heard his voice sound so tight and threatening. Even Jupiter had a funny look about him as he went for the hatchet. It was almost as if he was a stranger to us.

"Best be getting home now," said Winston, nodding toward the road.

Maudee reached for Possum's hand, and we took off out of the woods. We didn't even say good-bye to Winston and Jupiter, and Winston didn't say anything more to us, either. We never did find out about the light behind Tully's smokehouse. Maudee said it was lucky that she screamed, or Winston might have shot a possum after all (meaning her brother).

"Funny thing is," Possum said, "no one hunts possum this time of year."

"Why not?" Maudee asked.

"It's their breeding season, and they're all in their burrows. They don't come out till the weather turns cold." (Possum knows pretty much everything there is to know about possums.)

None of us said it aloud, but we were all wondering what Winston and Jupiter were doing out in the woods with a hatchet and a rifle if they weren't hunting. Things suddenly don't seem as simple in Sudbury as they used to.

Your brother, Levi

P.S. For getting home after dark, I received the punishment of having to pluck chickens for the quilting-bee supper. "Ain't folks tired of eating chicken all the time?" I groaned on hearing about it. But Miss Amelia showed no mercy. I can taste those chicken feathers in my mouth already.

Dear Austin,

Do you know how just when you think things aren't so good they suddenly turn worse than you could ever have imagined? That's how things are here. I was feeling put upon, what with all my plucking to do, when not two days later something far worse happened.

Darcy has disappeared! Kidnapped, we fear! And oh, Austin, it is all my fault.

Henry Fenton and his brother Will were in their orchard picking worms off the peaches when they saw Darcy pass by on her way home. Two men driving a green wagon pulled up alongside her, and Henry watched as Darcy climbed up into the wagon and drove off. That was the last time anyone saw her. They found one of her yellow ribbons on the road, but she never showed up at her house for supper that night.

Winston and Jupiter came by our place looking for her. Winston was frantic with worry, as the slave catchers had rented a wagon and some horses from

Charlie the blacksmith. Charlie only has one wagon that he rents out, and it is painted green.

Even though it was well after dark, Miss Amelia put on her bonnet and left in the wagon with Winston and Jupiter for Preacher Tully's place. She said that the preacher might have heard something. I don't know why she figured the preacher would know about it. I guess maybe it has something to do with his knowing so many people from church. As it turned out, Preacher Tully *had* heard some news — but it was all bad.

It seems that Mrs. Nolan, who sells butter to the preacher, also sells butter to some folks in town. One of her customers is Mrs. Simpson, and it was from Mrs. Simpson that she heard all about the slave catchers and that they were heading for North Carolina. Mrs. Simpson bragged to Mrs. Nolan that she had offered to do what she could to help the slave catchers "rid the area of riffraff." Although Mrs. Simpson didn't know anything about the two men they were hunting, she did tell them about a young girl. She told them the times that girl passed her house on her way into and out of town. She was telling them about Darcy!

So you can see why I am responsible, Austin. It was my idea for Darcy to visit Mrs. Simpson's window last month. If Darcy hadn't been there and Mrs. Simpson hadn't gotten so riled up, she might never have even thought to tell the slave catchers about Darcy at all. Winston and the preacher have left to look for her.

I keep remembering that day Possum and I were at Miller's store and what the men were saying about "black hides," and I shudder to think that those slave catchers would be looking at Darcy that way. What will happen to her without Jupiter and her pa there to protect her? Possum's pa says that she could get sold down into the Deep South, where they need slaves to bring in the cotton. He says that when slaves are swallowed up on those big plantations, they most likely won't be heard from again.

I had an awful nightmare last night, but at least I got to wake up from it and I was in my own bed. I can't help wondering where Darcy found herself waking up this morning.

I am sitting up in the hayloft now as I write this. The sun is setting over the cornfield, and the rays are pouring in through the loft window. It is the time of day when Jupiter, Possum, and I would take up our whittling. We'd be discussing the bumps on Plug Ugly's back, laughing and whispering, with Jupiter grinning as we whittled.

But there are no stories to listen to today and no laughing nor grinning neither. Jupiter hasn't come around, and I know why. He must blame me for what's happened to his sister, and truth be known, I'd feel the same way if I were him. If I could only somehow undo that one afternoon. I keep going over it in my head. I can hear us all talking, and I can see Darcy with her head full of those yellow ribbons.

Darcy's stick is leaning on a bale of hay where Jupiter left it, the little nightingale sitting atop it as silent as a stone.

Your brother, Levi

Dear Austin,

This letter brings good news and bad. The good news is that the Sudbury thieves have been caught! Turns out, Harley Rush's two older cousins, Tom and Amos, have been stealing supplies all over town for their journey out west. I reckon that mean streak of Harley's runs straight through the whole Rush family. The bad news is that the club members and I didn't get a chance to catch the thieves ourselves. It was Mr. Tanner who finally got 'em helping themselves to his smokehouse meats. In any case, it looks like those two crooks won't be joining you out west anytime soon.

And there's more bad news, Austin. Darcy is still missing. Possum's brother said that each day she's gone probably puts her that much farther away. I was glad that Jupiter was not there to hear this. I keep trying to think of something I could say to Jupe to help him feel better. But I reckon the only thing that would work would be the sound of Darcy's voice.

I heard a nightingale singing in the mulberry tree as I carried in the kindling this evening. I couldn't help wondering if Jupe will ever hear his nightingale again. If only Darcy had wings like that little bird in the mulberry tree! Then she could fly back to Sudbury, where she'd be safe.

That's what I'm praying for tonight. I'm praying to God that he sees fit to give Darcy wings or whatever miracle it takes to bring her back to us. I only hope he's listening.

Your brother, Levi

Dear Austin,

I am writing you this letter tonight, but I won't be able to get down to Miller's store to mail it until I return (and I don't know when that will be). I reckon you're going to be anxious about what I'm about to do, Austin, and Miss Amelia will be, too, when she finds out.

Preacher Tully and Winston got back yesterday. They were gone three weeks. They did not find Darcy, nor hear a solid lead about where she might be.

I was chopping wood today when Preacher Tully came by. I overheard him and Miss Amelia talking on the porch. Preacher Tully said that things were far worse than he had first thought, and that Miss Amelia must not repeat what he was about to tell her.

I moved in closer to hear.

"Winston was owned by a Simon Tate," the preacher said. "Before he died, Tate willed that Winston should have his freedom, but Winston's wife, Delia, and the children were not included in this stipulation. So when Simon Tate died, Winston was freed, but his family was now owned by Mary Tate, Simon's widow. She promptly sold them to her brother-in law, Henry Tate.

"It seems this Henry Tate was a meanspirited, evil man, and when he had Delia whipped to death, Winston took the children and ran. He ran with them all the way to Pennsylvania.

"So you see, Darcy and Jupiter are not free." The preacher sighed heavy here and ran his fingers through his hair. "They are still the property of Henry Tate. And that's not the worst of it. All we do know is that those slave catchers were from somewhere in North Carolina. We have no way of knowing who they were or where they might have taken Darcy. Without papers to prove she's a free person, our only hope of getting Darcy back is to buy her, but we'd have to find her first."

Oh, Austin, I never thought things could be so bad. When I heard Miss Amelia ask about Jupiter, I held my breath to hear, for the preacher had lowered his voice to a whisper.

"He is in danger as well. Winston knows how slim his chances are of finding Darcy now. He's decided to get Jupiter out of Pennsylvania while he still has a chance at freedom. Canada is their only hope.

"They'll leave tomorrow night. With the slave catchers running across the borders into the free states and carrying people off, Pennsylvania is no longer safe. They've got to go farther north."

I heard a horse and wheels and looked around the house to see Winston and Jupiter pulling up in their wagon. Winston's usually straight broad shoulders were slumped over, as if he had a heavy weight on them. His face was sadder than I've ever seen it. Jupiter was staring at the ground. I went over to the barn to wait for him.

Miss Amelia and the preacher went to talk to Winston, and Jupiter climbed down and came looking for me. We went up in the hayloft to be alone.

I told him all that I had heard, and how I would hate for him to have to go to Canada, but he shook his head.

"What do you mean, no?" I whispered. "If your

pa says, you've got to go, Jupe. What else can you do?"

Jupiter put his hand over his ear and then over his throat.

"Hear a song?" I whispered. I tried to figure out what he was telling me. Why did he want to hear a song now? Then he leaned over and picked up his walking stick.

"Darcy!" I cried. "You want to hear Darcy sing! But how?"

He walked over to the window and pointed to the road leading away from the house.

I knew then what he was planning. He was heading south rather than north. He was going to find Darcy! Once I understood this, I couldn't let him go alone. Now, you know that I've never been farther south than the Fentons' farm, and I don't know what North Carolina will be like, but I can't sit here in Sudbury doing nothing, knowing that I was responsible for Darcy's kidnapping in the first place.

So we hatched a plan to go together. The hard

79

part for Jupiter will be leaving Whistle behind, but it would be too dangerous to take him along. I packed a sack with some things we'll need—my slingshot, my flask of hiccup remedy, an old canteen for water, my knife, my flint rock for starting fires, some gingerbread in a napkin, and two pieces of rock candy. I'm also taking Reuben's old turnip head with me to work on when we've got time. I've put some sheets of paper into the sack as well. I'll write to you from the road and mail the letters when I return. I don't know when that will be, Austin, and I hope you won't be worrying too much in the meantime.

Jupiter is taking Darcy's walking stick with him. He aims to give it to her when we find her. Traveling south is such a dangerous thing for Jupiter to be doing, and I wonder at his courage. I only hope we have enough between us to do what we're setting out to do.

Nothing we ever did in our club seemed as serious as this. I wish we had spent more time working on being real daredevils and not just pretending. If ever I needed your advice, Austin, it's now. I wish you were here to tell me how to find the courage to be more than the hiccuppy coward of a boy I feel to be tonight.

Your brother, Levi

Dear Austin,

So much has happened, I don't know where to begin.
I suppose I should start with the night before last,
when Jupiter and I left Sudbury. We met up back of
the Hepples' cow barn after midnight and took off
through the woods. Neither of us knew how to get to
North Carolina. All we knew was that it was south of
Sudbury.

We walked toward the Fenton place, and when
we got there we just kept on going, following along
the canal. We slept out under some pine trees along
the bank, and the next morning we ate the gingerbread along with the rock candy for our breakfast.
After that, we walked along the canal until we
met a barge that was heading south. The bargeman
was friendly enough and offered to give us a ride
downstream. I asked if he had seen a young girl
with yellow ribbons and two men pass by, but he
had not.

Neither Jupiter nor I had ever been on a barge

afore, and it was great fun to glide along the water. We got off about ten miles downstream, and the man threw us each a potato from a barrel for our supper. We walked some till we grew tired.

As I write this I am sitting by a fire that we made from some birch twigs and brush. The sun is going down, and we're roasting our potatoes and some ears of corn that we picked from a farmer's field. I even found an old licorice stick in my pocket, which we decided to eat first. We were both grinning at our good fortune as we chomped on the hard licorice, when we heard an owl hooting in a sycamore tree over our heads. I looked over at Jupiter. The smile had left his face as his eyes searched the branches above us.

I knew who he was thinking of. I am thinking of her too.

"Could be they don't have any owls living down in the Carolinas," I said, trying to make him feel easier.

"Could be," his shrug seemed to answer. "Or could be they got worse," his eyes seemed to say.

We sat there for a long spell just watching the fire and listening to that owl hooting at the moon.

Your brother, Levi

Dear Austin,

We traveled clear on down into Virginia today, though I'm not sure what day it is. On the road you lose track of time. You also get mighty thirsty. We drank up a lot of the hiccup remedy, not on account of nerves but from thirst. I sure wish we hadn't done that. There's just enough to ward off one more fit, I reckon.

Got a ride from a schoolteacher by the name of Miss Milly Keck, who had a shiny black trap and a fine-looking bay. Miss Milly invited us to take a seat beside her, if we cared for a ride. This was no easy matter, as the seat was short and Miss Milly was on the bountiful side.

It was about noon from the looks of the sun and hotter than a day in July in Sudbury. We had drunk most of our water and so were much relieved to be given a ride. Lucky for us, Miss Milly was traveling almost forty miles to visit her ailing mother. When she asked where we were headed, I told her we were visiting family down south. She gave us a peculiar look but didn't say more.

When we stopped to rest and water the horse, Miss Milly reached for a basket at her feet. I nearly fainted with hunger when she opened it, for the smell of buttermilk and bacon biscuits was too good to be true. Having had nothing to eat since the night before, Jupiter and I could have eaten that whole basketful by ourselves.

But afore we had the chance to try, Miss Milly insisted that we offer some to "William first, as he'd be offended if we were to eat without him," she said.

Jupiter looked behind us, and I looked under our seat, as we were both wondering where this "William" could be hiding.

"He simply can't abide bad manners," Miss Milly continued, nodding toward her horse.

We turned our attention to the bay and then back down at the basket of biscuits. Neither of us had ever met a horse who cared one way or the other about manners, and we wondered just what that would look like. But Miss Milly didn't give us a chance to see, for she had already reached into the basket and was offering William a biscuit.

Then she told us how special a horse her William was and how he was named after a great poet. She recited a poem all about love and roses by an English fella called William Shakesomething. She said she liked his poetry so well that she had to name her horse after him. She reached back into the basket and fed William three more biscuits.

We finally parted company at a crossroads, and Miss Milly pointed to the road leading south and told us that "parting was such sweet sorrow."

I shook my head, not knowing how to answer, on account of I wasn't sure just what she was so sorry about. But I sure knew that I was sorry to see William eating all those buttermilk biscuits—especially since Jupe and I only got one apiece!

We walked till twilight and didn't meet anyone else on the road. In the woods we found a hollow that made a good bed. Jupiter is lying beside me, staring up at the sky. I wonder if he's thinking about Darcy again. I suppose he is. I'm thinking about her, too, and about Miss Amelia back home. I hope she isn't having any of those heart palpitations of hers, worrying about me. Well, the light is gone, and I best get some sleep for tomorrow's journey.

Your brother, Levi

Dear Austin,

It's been a while since I could sit down to write you. We hitched a ride on the back of a preacher's buggy that took us on a long and bumpy journey through the state of Virginia.

After that, we walked for a few miles afore coming upon a good-size pond. We found an old man sitting there in his wagon. He had driven his rig into the water to tighten his wheels. Jupiter and I decided to have a swim to cool off. The old man smiled and tipped his corn-shuck hat as we swam by him. Do you remember what Old Man Grissard looks like? This old fella had the same leathery-looking face and red nose.

He seemed friendly enough, sitting and picking at his teeth with a goose quill, but there was a curious smell about him. As we swam in closer to his wagon we could see that his leg was stretched out afore him with one pant leg rolled up. Bound to his leg with a string were two live toads!

"I expect it seems a curious sight," the old fella

89

spoke up. He went on to tell us that his name was Fergus T. McGrath, and he explained how he had been bitten by a copperhead that very morning.

"'Twas lucky for me I had my chickens in tow." He pointed to the crate of chickens in the back of his wagon. Fergus went on to tell us how he had killed one, slitting it down the middle, and then tied its entrails over the bite. When the chicken began to turn cold, he threw it off and caught the toads.

"Their bodies draw the venom out," Fergus explained as Jupiter and I stared bug-eyed at the toads, which still had some life left in them, for they would wiggle every now and then. I kept thinking of Plug Ugly and was glad that Possum was not there to witness their struggle.

When the toads finally died, Fergus untied the sorry-looking things and threw them into the water. He said his bite was all cured, and to celebrate he drove out of the pond and shared some dried beef and cottonseed tea with us.

"Be still, oh, mah heart," I said as I got a whiff of the dried beef.

Jupiter looked at me and grinned. We were both thinking of Possum then.

"Be still, oh, mah heart!" Fergus repeated. "Sounds like a song."

Then he pulled a mouth harp out of his pocket and began to play. Every once in a while he'd stop and start to sing, "Be still, oh, mah heart, my gal and I had to part…" It went on and on like that, with lots of good rhymes.

We traveled with Fergus T. McGrath in his wagon for the next two days. He told us some good tales, and he knew lots of songs. But as much as we enjoyed his singing and his stories, I have to admit that we were not sorry to leave him, for the company he kept was hard on the nose. After sharing a wagon with a crate of chickens, three piglets, and six ducks, the smell was mighty powerful.

We had confided in Fergus all about Darcy and how we hoped to find her. He told us about a slave auction "some five miles south of here," where we might look for her. "But you must be careful. And Jupiter here best not do the looking," he cautioned.

He said he wished he could take us there himself, but he had pigs to sell. We understood and promised to be careful.

When we parted ways, Fergus seemed concerned and wouldn't let us go without giving us the rest of the dried beef, two turnips, and an onion.

I felt so grateful for all that he had done for us that I wanted to give him something. The only thing I had was old turnip head. (I will make another one for Reuben, I promise.) Fergus laughed when I put the stick into his wagon and said that it was the best exchange of turnips he'd ever had!

By the time he let us off, the critters' stink was all over our clothes, and we were desperate to find a crick or river to dunk ourselves in. We walked for a couple of miles but didn't find one. As it turned out, that was lucky for us.

What we did find were three young men who were sitting in the shade of a locust tree. At first I was hoping that they might offer us something to eat, but when we got up closer to them, I could see that they had been sucking on a jug for a spell.

"Now, take a looky here," one of them called out on seeing us. He had a round pockmarked face under a straw hat and poppy eyes that reminded me of Plug Ugly.

"Who might this little master and his slave be come walking our way?" he taunted. At first I thought they might be all gurgle and no guts, so Jupiter and I just kept on walking.

"Now, you two stop right there," the man with Plug Ugly's eyes barked so loud that my hair stood on end. The others both turned to look at us as we stopped dead center in the road.

"He don't resemble a Muller nor an Ingram neither," another of them said. "Whose house you from, boy? Who's your daddy? I don't recognize your features none."

I tried to think of how I should answer this, but afore I could, the tallest man stood up and put his hand on the other man's shoulder as he waved the jug in his hand.

"It's of no consequence, John Lee, whose house he might come from. He's a guest passing through

Horn lands, and 'shaw, our mama has taught us our manners. Why, it would be downright unmannerly of us boys not to offer 'em some refreshment." The other two laughed at this and got to their feet.

"Looks as if his darky could use a little contentment," one of the men said in a gargly voice as he pointed to Jupiter.

"O' course, we can't have him holding the jug to his mouth," he snarled. "That would never do. No, sir, that would ruin the whole batch of this here sweet contentment for any of us."

"We'll just have to pour some into him," the man called John Lee said as he took a wobbly step toward us.

I was trying to figure which way we should run, but they had surrounded us. I could see Jupiter's nails digging into his walking stick as we inched closer to each other. I hiccupped real loud, and one of the men began to laugh. I quick put my hand over my back pocket. Somehow just holding my hand over the flask calmed me enough to keep a fit from coming on. But there was nothing to calm my knees, for they had begun to buckle beneath me so that I didn't know if I even could run!

But just when it looked as if we were done for, the wind picked up and the man closest to us let out a holler.

"'Shaw, they got a powerful stink on them!" he cried, backing away from us. The other two pretty much followed suit, coming closer, then backing off as soon as they got a good whiff. That's when I found that my knees worked just fine! We ran off the road and into the woods, and we didn't stop running till our sides hurt. Jupiter was so shook up his teeth were chattering, and I was trying hard not to cry.

After meeting with those bad fellas, we decided it was too dangerous to travel by the road. We'd have to stick to the woods instead. We found a crick and were able to wash the stink off, though we were both wondering if maybe we ought to leave it on, as it served us so well!

The only thing that kept me from crying today was thinking of you, Austin. You're the bravest brother a boy could have, going out alone to Oregon like you did. And so I kept them tears back behind my eyes, 'cause I don't want you to ever have to be disappointed in me. I want to be as strong on this trip as you were on yours. You always told me how brave Pa was and how we each had some of him in us. I think you got more than I do, but even with the little bit I got, I aim to use it to make him proud.

Oh, I know Pa's gone, but sometimes I think about what Preacher Tully says about good souls going to heaven. And I think about Pa looking down from his place in heaven, and Ma there with him, listening out for us. And I imagine Pa smiling, 'cepting when he hears a hiccup.

Your brother, Levi

Dear Austin,

I'm not sure what day it is, as we've been walking for so long the days and nights seem to run into one another. We've been living on berries and nuts and not much more. I never knew the state of North Carolina was so big! I guess Jupiter and I just figured once we got here we'd find Darcy right off. Never thought about *not* finding her. Jupiter's shoes are almost worn through, and we're both bit up and bloodied with chigger bites, poison ivy, and beggar's-lice.

We can't seem to find our way out of these woods. If we ever do make it back to Sudbury, I don't suppose I will ever set foot out of Pennsylvania again, 'cepting to come out to live with you. I sure wish you could be here now, as I know you'd probably find a way to get us out of here.

The nights are the worst, as these woods are full of strange-sounding birds and critters. It's the critters that give us concern. You can feel their eyes on you at night. Jupiter is most afeared of snakes, but I'm on the lookout for panthers myself.

I knew it was a bad idea as soon as I started, but I found myself telling ghost stories around the fire a few nights back. I told my favorite one about old Bloody Head, and then Jupiter clicked his teeth to let me know that he wanted to hear the one about old Rattle Bones. When the trees creaked in the wind over our heads, we knew it weren't really the trees at all. We knew it was old Rattle Bones come looking to pick our bones clean.

And when we heard some critter in the brush, we were certain it was old Bloody Head come to fetch our heads for his collection! We've been sleeping with our shoes on ever since and doing a powerful lot of praying.

Your brother, Levi,
lost somewhere in the wilds of the Carolinas

Dear Austin,

Still hungry, still scratching chiggers, and still lost…
I don't feel much like writing, but it's the only way I
have to somehow feel as if we're talking. Oh, Austin,
I'd give anything to hear your voice right now. If
only you could tell me what to do. I wonder what
you're doing at this very moment when I'm feeling so
low. Are you laughing over a joke Reuben just told?
Are you whistling one of your tunes? Are you sleeping? Are you smiling? Are you listening?

Your brother, Levi

Dear Austin,

Our big worry now, aside from having so little to eat, is gators. We found our way out of the woods and into a swamp. Jupiter and I both remembered the story that his pa told us all 'bout how gators eat folks alive down in the swamps. They've got some strange-looking bugs here and moss that hangs from the trees, all of which gives me a most uneasy feeling.

When we finally got to drier ground, we found some good pine knots, which we used to start a fire last night, but there were no vittles to cook over it and we went to bed mighty hungry. As it turned out, hunger was the least of our troubles, for no sooner had I fallen asleep than I was woken by the loud click of a peppercorn pistol nuzzling the side of my head!

I got a whiff of lead by my nose and the feel of hard cold metal nudging me just above my right ear. I blinked, and when my eyes got adjusted to the darkness, I could see a black face frowning afore me.

There was a deep voice to go with the face, and it rumbled in my ears.

"Who you be?"

It had been so long since I'd heard another human voice, I didn't know what to make of it. But it didn't take me long to realize that this voice was not friendly.

"Levi Ives," I gulped as the man pressed the pistol tighter against my skull.

"And you?" he whispered to Jupiter in a manner just as threatening.

"He can't answer," I replied.

"Why not?" the voice demanded.

"He got the words scared out of him," I said, my own words coming out mighty quivery.

"And his name?"

"Jupiter," I croaked. "Jupiter Hale."

The pressure of the revolver against my head lessened a bit as the man paused, then repeated, "Hale? Hale? Y'all know who yah daddy be?"

Jupiter nodded as his breaths came in fits and starts.

"Winston," I spoke up. "His pa is Winston Hale."

"Why, I knew of a Winston Hale married to a Delia on de Tate plantation in de state of Maryland. Had dem a baby called Jupiter. Don't tell, you be dat baby!" His voice suddenly grew friendlier, and he lowered his pistol.

I gulped a breath of air, relieved to have the gun away from my head. Jupiter and I slowly sat up. When we did, we could see two men standing in back of the man with the gun. Their faces were all black as the night, and they looked as frightened as we were.

"Last time I heard 'bout yah daddy," the man continued, "heard he be runnin' a route up in de state of Pennsylvania. Work wit some preacher. Would dat be de same Winston Hale?"

Jupiter nodded.

"Preacher Tully was de name, if I remember," the man said. "He and your daddy be deliverin' slaves goin' on up into Canada."

I turned to look at Jupiter, wondering what the

man was talking about, when I realized that he meant the Underground Railroad!

"Your pa and Preacher Tully?" I gasped, staring in disbelief.

Jupiter had a strange look on his face, and I suddenly remembered the last time I had seen that look—out in the woods back of Preacher Tully's smokehouse the night I was with Possum and Maudee, investigating the strange light.

I was so stunned it was all I could do to keep my mouth from dropping open in disbelief. But there was little time to ponder it all, for the man with the pistol had suddenly begun to snore! It was the strangest thing, Austin, for he was standing up afore us when his eyes suddenly closed and he fell asleep, sound asleep standing on two feet, just as if he were lying on a bed.

"Mercy, Moses, you havin' a sleepin' spell agin?" one of the other men asked.

"Moses?" I whispered. "Did you say Moses?"

"She be our Moses, all right," the man replied.

"Bringin' her people out of de dark into de light to de promised land. We runnin' from Marster Rankin's bullwhip, and without Moses here, we most likely never git past his dogs."

"Don't know many folk, man or woman, willin' to take on dose devil dogs," the other man whispered.

So the sleeping man called Moses was not a man at all but a woman! Her voice was so low she sounded like a man. That's when I remembered the woman conductor on the Underground Railroad that Miss Amelia had told me about. Her name was Harriet Tubman, but her nickname was Moses. I wondered if this could be the same Moses.

Then as suddenly as she had fallen asleep, the woman woke up with a grunt and began to speak as if no time had gone by at all.

"So, Levi Ives, you tell me jest what you and Jupiter Hale be doin' down here in dis slave state."

I tried to explain about Darcy and how we had hoped to find her and bring her home with us to

106

Sudbury. I also told Moses about the men with the jug and how we came to be hiding in the woods.

"Come Saturday der be a big slave auction takin' place on de Meriweather plantation not two miles south of here," one of the men said. "Most likely dem slave catchers be headin' there. Traders come from miles around to sell wat dey buy and wat dey ketch. It be jest beyond dat crick." He pointed to a crick that ran to our right. It must have been the auction that Fergus had mentioned.

Moses shot Jupiter a look, and she frowned. "I know'd wat you be thinkin', but listen up, now. Ain't no way you two half-mites could free a horse fly once it be put on de auction block. So puts it out of yah head. 'Sides, yah daddy knows y'all even down here?"

Jupiter lowered his head and shifted from one foot to the other.

After much hesitation, he shook his head.

"Mercy, dat be a foolish thing you done!" Moses sighed. "Actin' mo' like Jupiter de baby den Jupiter de boy. Like to drive yah daddy wild wit worry! Don't yah know yah gots to have a pass to git through dese lands? Witout dat pass dey whup de hide right off yah black back faster den yah can shuck an ear o' corn. And now yah got de Marster John Lee Horn lookin' fer y'all. He find us wit you and he likes to lynch de lot of us!"

Jupiter dropped his eyes to the ground, and I knew how bad he was feeling, for it did seem as if we were in a heap of trouble. Moses took off her hat and scratched at the scarf around her head.

"We'll rest fer a bit," she whispered. "But only a little bit. Dis here be Horn land, and de sooner we be off it, de safer we be. You two comin' wit us now," she said, turning back to Jupiter and me. "I'll git y'all as far as Philadelphia, and den we sees 'bout gettin' in touch wit yah people. I'll send word to de folks I know and see if dey heard anythin' 'bout yah sister."

She reached under her coat and pulled out two pieces of hardtack, which she handed to us. I thought I would die of happiness at getting something to eat other than nuts and berries.

As the others lay on the ground to rest, one of the men asked Moses if she had a map to guide her to Philadelphia. She laughed at this and said she didn't "need no maps. All's I needs is shinin' above our heads," she whispered, pointing up to a bright star in the sky. I knew it was the North Star on account of its brightness.

"It's God's light shinin' down to guide our way," she said. Her voice, though deep, had grown suddenly softer and more like a woman's as we sat staring up at the starlight through the trees.

Moses went on to tell us about the cricks she knew that ran north and how if she got away from them and too far into the woods, she used the moss that grew on the north sides of the trees to guide her.

"So you see," she said, smiling, "the good Lord gives us all de map we needs to finds our way to freedom."

"Amen," one of the men whispered, and I found myself thinking "amen" along with him. I don't know how long we could have lasted, lost like we were. I supposed Moses was right about our not being able to save Darcy, and I was grateful that we had run into someone as smart and brave as Moses to lead us back home.

Now, if only Jupiter had been thinking like me, things might have turned out different. As it was, those were nearly the last words we were to hear from the woman called Moses, and the last moments we were to have the comfort of her protection. The light is leaving, and I will continue when I can.

Your brother, Levi

Dear Austin,

I fear Moses was right. Jupiter and I couldn't free a horse fly from the likes of this place. Oh, Austin, it's a terrible business, this selling of people. I suppose I should first tell you how we came to leave Moses and her group.

Everyone was dozing, and the minute Moses shut her eyes Jupiter signaled to me. I didn't know what he had in mind, but I did know he wanted me to follow him. So up we got, and I stayed close behind as Jupiter tiptoed past the silent group.

"Wer you headed?" a deep voice suddenly purred.

We turned back to see Moses reaching for her gun in the moonlight.

Jupiter latched on to my arm and grabbed the front of his britches.

"Uh, h-he's got to relieve himself," I stammered. "And he's afeared of snakes, so I have to go along," I quickly added.

Moses nodded but held on to the gun. "Don't stray too far."

When we had made our way behind some bushes, I unbuttoned my britches. "How'd you know I had to go?" I asked Jupiter, who was standing beside me.

He seemed impatient and pointed to a stand of pines that ran along the crick.

"What's over there?" I asked.

Jupiter brought his finger to my lips to silence me. Then he pointed to me and to himself and back to the crick.

"Are you saying that you want us to leave?" I whispered.

He quickly nodded in agreement.

"But Jupe, you heard what she said."

I tried to persuade him to go back with me to Moses and the others, but he looked me in the eye and did the only thing that could have shut me up. He reached into his back pocket and pulled out a little scrap of yellow hair ribbon.

One look at that ribbon was all I needed. I knew

he could never leave her alone down here, not after hearing about the whip and those "devil dogs."

"We best hurry afore they come looking for us," I whispered.

And that's how we came to be back on our own, heading south again! At least this time we had some idea of which way to go. One of the men had said that the auction was two miles south of the crick. Following Moses' map, we found the North Star and figured which way south was. We took off for the crick, running as fast as we could. Every now and then we'd stop to catch our breath and listen. We did hear voices once, but they sounded far off, and we knew they'd be heading in the opposite direction.

We didn't make the full two miles that night, as the woods were so overgrown it was slow going. Along the way I couldn't stop thinking about Winston, the preacher, and the Underground Railroad.

As I started to piece things together, I began to think aloud about Miss Amelia.

"I always wondered how she came to know so

much about the Underground Railroad. And if she and the preacher were really sweet on each other, wouldn't he have told her about it? And maybe she had even helped!"

That's when it dawned on me.

"All those pies!" I suddenly cried.

Jupiter shot me a guilty look.

"Miss Amelia's pies weren't just for the preacher and his pa, were they? She was baking for the railroad, wasn't she?"

Jupiter nodded.

It suddenly all made perfect sense and yet made no sense, if you know what I mean. Can you believe it, Austin? Our own Miss Amelia working for the Underground Railroad!

I couldn't get it all out of my head, and I felt cheated somehow, cheated that Miss Amelia hadn't told me herself. But as hurt as I was over Miss Amelia's secret, I didn't have time to think on it much the next day.

At sunup the next morning, we woke with the birds that had started to sing in the branches of the trees over our heads. We found some berries to eat, but after the hardtack, my stomach was aching for real food. We were able to find the road that ran above the crick, and we followed it south, careful to keep out of sight.

After a few hours we heard horses, wagon wheels, and singing. It weren't happy singing but rather a low, mournful tune. When we crept up to the edge of the woods, we could see wagons filled with slaves rolling over the dusty road. Young and old, men and women, boys and girls, and babies sleeping in their mothers' arms. Many of the men were in chains, and some had big iron collars around their necks.

They were herded into the wagons like cattle. Most were quiet, but a few were singing. We followed along, keeping to the bushes, until we reached a pebbled drive that ran into a yard. From the bushes we could see all manner of buggies, traps, and wagons parked at the hitching posts. There were sheds and pens, and crowds of people were gathered around platforms raised off the ground. I told

Jupiter that he dare not come any farther, for if any of those slave traders saw him, there was no telling what would happen.

We agreed that he would stay hidden in the bushes behind a shed while I went into the yard to look for Darcy. I promised that I'd get back to him and we would somehow figure out what to do next if I found her. But the farther I walked into the yard, the more uncertain I became that we would ever figure a way out.

The first thing I passed was a platform that held a large set of scales. A man in chains stepped onto it to be weighed. The man reminded me of Winston. He was tall and strong; only his eyes were different. They stared out at the crowd, blank and empty, as if they were looking right through the people, not seeing anything at all.

"One hundred seventy-five pounds plus chain. Let the bidding start at seven dollars a pound!" the white man beside him shouted.

"I'll give you five hundred!" a heavyset man in a wide leather hat called.

"Why, I couldn't let him go at that price," the auctioneer replied, spitting a plug of tobacco off the platform. "Just have a look at his back," he said, turning the man around and pulling up his shirt. "Those are old scars. This buck had the wildness whipped out of him long ago. He's been broken in, and all you have to do is set him down in your fields. Why, he's been bred for the fields, can't y'all see that? Who'll give me eight hundred dollars?"

I hurried past them and came to a row of pens. I was expecting to see pigs or cattle in them, but instead they were filled with people! The stench and dirt was something terrible. There were babies crying, whips cracking, men shouting out bids and spitting juice. A woman was pleading not to be separated from her children, and there was a boy about your age whose back was so scarred from whip marks I had to turn away and could not look.

I kept searching for Darcy, hoping to catch sight of those yellow ribbons of hers. I stood watching and waiting as a pen was opened and an overseer cracked his big blacksnake whip.

"Halls," he shouted. "Elizabeth, Nell, and Parilee."

A woman came out of the pen with two little girls. The overseer cracked the whip beside the woman's feet, and she nearly jumped onto the platform. The little girls held on to her skirts.

"Now, we can sell 'em as a lot, two thousand dollars, or we can split 'em up," the auctioneer called. "You're lookin' at a healthy breeding wench, not a day over twenty. Take the young 'uns as a pair, to be raised up for the house or field or however you can use 'em."

The little girls clung to their mother, with their heads buried in her skirts.

A trader stepped up to the platform and put on a pair of white gloves. He nodded to the woman, and the overseer cracked his whip.

"Open your mouth," the auctioneer barked.

The woman opened her mouth, and the trader ran his fingers over her teeth, just like he was examining a horse.

"Cupworms in her teeth," the trader grumbled out loud. "She's closer to thirty than twenty. I'll give you five hundred for her, but I don't need the rest."

"Do I hear six hundred?" the auctioneer shouted. The woman began to sob and shake, and the little girls started to cry as they were pulled from her. I felt my stomach tighten into knots as I realized the only thing that was keeping me from being up there on that auction block was the whiteness of my skin. And you know, Austin, I looked down at my hands then, my white hands, and I felt such shame.

"Son, if you ain't buying, you best make room for one who is," a bearded man growled as he leaned beside me. His breath was hot and smelled of whiskey.

I stepped to the side and heard a young girl's voice call, "Levi!"

I spun around to see a dirty canvas curtain pinned over a set of stalls. I heard the voice again, but I couldn't make out the words. Was she calling "Levi" or "Eli"? Was it Darcy or someone who sounded like her? There were so many voices and so much noise it was impossible to tell.

"Darcy," I shouted. "Darcy, are you in there?" I suddenly recalled all the times I had told her to hush up, all the times I had wished she'd leave us alone and stop making so much noise, and I felt my heart twist in my chest at the memory.

"Darcy!" I pleaded. "It's me, Levi. Just let me know if you're there."

I couldn't see the faces inside the stalls, and the overseer told me, "Move aside, and stop disturbing the stock." Then he cracked his whip and lifted the curtain.

"Stock"—that's how they think of them. That's how they were thinking of Darcy. How could these men, these grown men, be so wrongheaded, Austin? How does that happen? I may only be a boy, but I know the difference between an animal and a little girl. And to be truthful, Austin, these men were treating these people worse than animals.

I stood on the edge of a trough so I could get a good look, but there were too many people packed in and not enough time to see them all afore the curtain came back down. The voice I had thought to be Darcy's was lost in all of the shouting and sobbing.

120

When I realized that there were at least ten of these pens and platforms, with bidding going on all at the same time, my hopes sank. How could I watch all of them? How was I ever to find Darcy—if she was here? I dreaded going back to Jupiter with this news. But I knew he'd be anxious by now, and so I headed back to the bushes where I'd left him.

But when I got there, he was gone! I searched everywhere but couldn't find him. I was desperate with worry, and my head was reeling with questions. Had he gotten scared and decided to wait back in the woods? Had he hoped to hook back up with Moses and her group? Why hadn't he waited for me? It wasn't long afore I had my answers, for as I stood with my back to a platform, I heard an auctioneer call out:

"What'll you give fer this healthy-looking young buck? Why, jest look at his back. Not a mark on it, no sir."

I was about to walk away when I heard the auctioneer's excited voice declare, "And he comes with this here finely carved walking stick—bet he worked

121

it himself. Why, this little bird at the top looks like it's ready to take to the sky. That's a talent with wood, that is. Just how talented are you, young buck? Let's see how talented you are with your feet. Can you dance for these fine folks?" The overseer cracked his whip and the crowd roared with laughter.

Stunned, I turned my head in time to see the auctioneer waving Darcy's walking stick in the air. And beside him on the platform stood Jupiter, stripped to the waist, his eyes wide with fear as the overseer's whip cracked across his legs.

"Oh, Jupe!" I cried. "Oh, no! Oh, no!"

I am out of paper and can write no more.

Levi

Dear Austin,

I found this auction bill and so am writing you a letter on the back. Jupiter was about to be sold off, and there was nothing I could do to stop it.

"He's not a buck! He's a boy!" I shouted at the auctioneer. "He's a boy, and he's got a name. His name is Jupiter Hale."

I felt my heart pounding against my chest as everyone turned to stare at me.

"Well, thank you, son, fer that powerful piece of information." The auctioneer flashed a smile, but I could see his anger boiling behind his grin. "Truth is, this ain't no church social, so if you ain't biddin', you best keep quiet, lest you get mixed up with those that are."

They don't want to know him, I thought as two men beside me stepped forward to get a closer look. They don't want to know him at all.

He's Jupiter! I wanted to shout at them. He can talk without words. He's got a dog called Whistle and a sister named Darcy. He can dive off Widow's

Rock and whittle better than anyone I know. He's afraid of snakes, but he's brave enough to walk through a swamp full of them and gators, too.

But I didn't say any of those things. Instead I just stood there silent and helpless as the auctioneer started the bidding again. My eyes shot back to Jupiter, whose forehead was beading with sweat. His eyes were big and glassy with fear, and he was trembling badly.

If only we had stayed home, Jupe, I thought. If only we had stayed home.

But we were a long way from Sudbury. He was standing up there all alone, just as he had done at Widow's Rock. Only this was worse, much worse, because this wasn't going to end with one dive. This could go on and on for the rest of his life! I remembered Possum's brother telling us about the slaves sold to the cotton fields and how badly they were treated. How their entire lives were used up and spent under the lash of an overseer's bullwhip. I shuddered at the thought of Jupiter's life taken away from him like that.

A man beside me called out, "Three hundred dollars." A voice in the back of the crowd called out, "Four."

"I have four, do I hear five?" the auctioneer shouted.

Jupiter bit down on his lip as the overseer tugged on the rope that bound his hands. I felt a fit of hiccups coming on, but I shook them off. Jupiter was doing his best to stay strong, and I had to do the same.

"Four going once, going twice…"

My eyes filled with tears, so that I couldn't see.

"Be still, oh, mah heart," a voice suddenly sang out from the back of the crowd. "I'll give you five hundred dollars."

"Sold!" the auctioneer declared, lowering his gavel on the wooden podium in front of him.

I climbed back up on the edge of a water trough and was able to see the crowd parting as men tried to steer clear of the latest buyer. A buyer wearing a corn-shuck hat and carrying a powerful stink on him!

"Fergus!" I cried, jumping off the trough.

For it was Fergus! Fergus T. McGrath himself, who had bid on and bought Jupiter for five hundred dollars! And you know, Austin, I didn't care how bad he smelled. He was the sweetest sight I ever laid eyes on, and I told him so.

We made our way up to the platform to free Jupiter, and while I used my knife to cut the ropes around his wrists, Fergus dealt with the auctioneer, who would not let go of Darcy's walking stick. I think the stink on Fergus was so strong that the auctioneer finally gave it up in desperation just to be rid of him. Just then a strong black hand reached out for Jupiter, and I looked up to see Winston standing afore us! Preacher Tully was at his side. That's when we discovered that it wasn't Fergus who had put up the money to buy Jupiter, but rather Winston and Preacher Tully!

The preacher explained it all. He told us how he and Winston had come down looking for us. They had made it all the way into the state of North Carolina when the axle on the preacher's wagon broke. A short spell later Fergus stopped by to offer his help. But the axle was beyond anything they could repair, so Fergus offered to give Winston and the preacher a lift to the nearest town.

It wasn't until they had gotten into the back of the wagon that Winston recognized my old turnip head sticking out from behind the crate of chickens!

When the preacher questioned Fergus, he told them of our meeting and where he thought we might be headed. Winston and the preacher begged him to take them to the auction, and he agreed on the condition that they buy the chickens, pigs, and ducks he had meant to sell.

Winston held on to Jupiter now as if he would never let him go. We were laughing and crying and so relieved to see one another. Only when Winston asked about Darcy did we all quiet down.

I told him we hadn't seen or heard of her, and he sighed so heavy I had to look away. After the preacher and Winston had searched the yard once more, we left in Fergus's wagon. This was no place for Winston or Jupiter to linger.

Riding away from that auction yard was like riding away from a funeral, for we all knew that riding north meant that we were riding away from any chance of finding Darcy.

Jupiter closed his eyes as soon as we got into the wagon. He didn't open them once till we were a mile or more away. I don't ever want to see or hear or smell the likes of that evil place again. I know Jupiter must feel the same, but I don't imagine he could ever forget it. The lash marks on his legs aren't likely to let him.

Your brother, Levi, heading home

Dear Austin,

I am writing you from the hayloft of our barn. I've been back in Sudbury for almost a month. Maybe by now you've gotten my letters from the Underground Railroad, which I sent when I came home. Miss Amelia was so glad to see me safe and sound, she didn't mention any chicken-plucking punishments until the day after I returned!

I've been coming up to the loft after school to work on a new walking stick for Reuben. Possum comes when he can, but it's not the same with Jupiter gone. He and Winston left for Canada two days after we got back. The preacher took them as far as New York State in his wagon. They most likely will never return, and I doubt that we shall ever meet again. Neither Jupiter nor his pa can read or write, never having been allowed to learn, so I don't expect a letter. There wasn't much of a good-bye. Miss Amelia says their hearts were too broken with losing Darcy.

Everything is different with them gone. I'm different, too, I guess. I can't pluck a chicken without sticking a feather behind my ear for luck. I can't look at the widow's summer kitchen without hoping to hear a song. I can't listen to the hoot of the barn owl at twilight without pausing to wonder. How are they all? How bitter cold is it way up in Canada? How punishing is the heat down south? Why is it that this had to happen? How will their hearts ever mend? How will it ever end?

Miss Amelia has decided to come out with me to Oregon come spring. She said she has to keep her promise to Pa to look out for us and that considering my disposition for poking my nose into troublesome places, she'd best keep an eye on me as I travel across the country. She is planning to return eventually to continue her work with Preacher Tully. Personally, I think Miss Amelia just wants to meet face to face the man whose recipe for gooseberry pie won her first place at the church social. So tell Reuben to look out for us!

Miss Amelia is already fixing to make me a new

set of clothes for the trip, as I've outgrown most of my britches. I suppose I outgrew a lot of things this summer, and you might not even recognize me when I get off that wagon train. Just like Miss Amelia predicted, I've outgrown my hiccup fits.

I was hoping that I'd outgrow being afraid, but I don't hope for that anymore. There's a lot to be afraid of in this world, Austin. I found that out this summer. But as much evil as there is out there, there's goodness, too, enough goodness to steady you and to keep the hiccups away, I guess.

Even my dreams are different now. I don't have such bad nightmares anymore, the way I used to. Each night as I lie in bed with my eyes closed, I call up the memory of a wagon heading north. Winston is at the reins with the preacher beside him. Jupiter and Whistle are sitting behind them. Whistle is the only one looking back. There isn't much baggage — just one basket, one trunk, and one little hickory stick poking up from between them, holding the likes of a small bird. Lately I've been dreaming about that little wooden nightingale. I see its stiff feathered

wings begin to flutter. I hear the soft, sad song it starts to sing. And I hear my own voice whisper, "Be still, oh, mah heart…Be still…"

Your brother, Levi

May 16, 1873

Dear Mr. Levi Ives,

I am writing to you in hopes that you will be able to help me locate my father, Winston Hale, and my brother, Jupiter John Hale. I have written to the Hepple family of Sudbury, Pennsylvania, but all my letters have gone unanswered. I fear they are either dead or have moved away. I have also written to Miss Amelia Cole, only to learn that she passed away in '71. And I have finally found you, my last hope.

I doubt that you would remember me, it being twenty years since I lived in Sudbury, but I pray that you might remember my brother and father. They lived and worked for Sirus Hepple. My father was a tall Negro man with scars along the side of his face. My brother Jupiter was mute. I have not seen or heard from either of them these last twenty years and do not know if they are still alive.

I would be most grateful if you could give me any

information on their whereabouts, as I am anxious to find them. I am living in the state of Alabama with my husband and three children. I have included my address on a separate paper.

If I may be so bold to tell you, Mr. Ives, while you probably have little memory of me, I remember you and your Miss Amelia quite well. I was sorry to hear of her passing. What I remember most is your friendship with my brother, and I must call upon that friendship now to aid my cause. If Jupiter is alive and you know his whereabouts, please write to me or send word to him that his sister, Darcy, is hoping to find him.

Yours truly,
Darcy Mellon

On July 14, 1873, in the town of Harper, Alabama, three little girls excitedly gathered around a wooden kitchen table as their mother tore open a package wrapped in brown paper. The postmark on the package read AUBURN, CANADA. Inside they discovered a letter and a small stick made of hickory. It appeared to be a walking stick, but quite short, as if made for a child. On the handle was carved a small bird.

Laughing and giggling, the little girls took turns holding the stick and walking around the room as their mother pored over the letter.

"What kind of bird do you suppose it's meant to be?" Neddy, the eldest girl, asked.

"Maybe it's a dove," her sister Pearl suggested.

"Or could be a sparrow," Etta May, the youngest, guessed.

"No," their mother finally whispered as she dropped the letter into her lap and with trembling hands reached for the little stick. She ran her long fingers over the delicately carved wings. Then she looked back at her daughters, with their big dark eyes, their ribboned hair, and their smiling faces.

"It's meant to be a nightingale," she told them as a tear rolled down her cheek. "Yes, a nightingale," she said in a voice so soft and low none but she could hear.

ELVIRA WOODRUFF is the author of more than a dozen picture books and novels for young readers, including *Dear Levi: Letters from the Overland Trail*, *The Orphan of Ellis Island*, and *George Washington's Socks*. She lives in Martins Creek, Pennsylvania.

NANCY CARPENTER has illustrated many books for children, including *Loud Emily* by Alexis O'Neill, *A Sister's Wish* by Kate Jacobs, and *Sitti's Secrets* by Naomi Shihab Nye, winner of the Jane Addams Picture Book Award. She makes her home in Brooklyn, New York.